The Ghost Boy

by Anne Schraff

Perfection Learning® Corporation
Logan, Iowa 51546

For information, contact:
Perfection Learning® Corporation
1000 North Second Avenue, P.O. Box 500,
Logan, Iowa 51546-0500.
Phone: 1-800-831-4190 • Fax: 1-800-543-2745
perfectionlearning.com

Paperback
ISBN-10: 0-7891-7538-X
ISBN-13: 978-0-7891-7538-0

Reinforced Library Binding
ISBN-10: 0-7569-8378-9
ISBN-13: 978-0-7569-8378-9

29998
3 4 5 6 PP 16 15 14 13

1

I WOKE UP suddenly. Something had startled me, but what was it?

I got up as quietly as possible and went to the cabin window. It was snowing outside. Large, soft-white snowflakes were sifting to earth.

Then I saw it—a face, a boy's face, looking straight at me!

I saw him for just an instant. He seemed to be all huge dark eyes, wild hair, and smoky skin.

Then he was gone. For a minute or more, I stared at the empty window.

My stepfather was suddenly by my side. I hadn't seen him get out of his sleeping bag or even heard him approach. Yet there he was, wide-awake.

"Tricia?" he said softly.

I was mixed-up and frightened. I wasn't sure what I'd just seen. I thought maybe it was a bad dream. Deep down inside, however, I knew I'd really seen someone at that cabin window.

My stepfather asked, "What's the matter, Tricia? You're shaking."

"I don't know, Lonnie," I said.

My stepfather's name is Lonnie Boone. A weird name, Lonnie, and one of the littler things I don't like about him.

But mainly I don't like Lonnie because he is my stepfather. Ever since my father died when I was seven, it had been just Mom, Doug, and me. Doug is my twelve-year-old brother. It seemed to me we managed just fine by ourselves.

Then along came Lonnie Boone and butted his way into our lives. What did we need him for?

"You must have had a bad dream," Lonnie said. With that he went back to his sleeping bag. And I sat back down on my cot in the dark cabin.

This cabin—it had been Lonnie's even before he married Mom. It was the last place I wanted to be right now. How I wished I were in Philadelphia instead with Mom and Aunt Sue and her new baby.

But Mom had loved the idea of shipping

Doug and me up here with Lonnie. "Tricia, you'll have a great time," she'd said.

"Yeah," Doug had agreed. He had liked the idea right from the start. "We can mess around in the snow and maybe learn to ski, too."

"I'd rather come with you to help Aunt Sue," I had insisted.

Mom had given me a funny look. That look told me it was no use nagging her to go to Philadelphia. She wanted us to get to know her new husband better.

That was Lonnie's little plan, too. When we first got to the cabin, he had said to me, "Your mom wants us to get to be good friends, Tricia."

"I didn't know that we were enemies," I said, hoping that would end the discussion. It didn't.

"We aren't. But we aren't friends either," he said.

I'd thought to myself, "And we won't ever be!"

Thinking about Lonnie took my mind off what I had seen for a while. Now that I was calmer, I felt tired. I told myself it was all a bad dream and went back to sleep.

But the next morning, the face in the window still haunted me. I couldn't hide behind lies. It hadn't been a dream.

I decided to talk to Doug about it. I found him outside, making a snowball.

"If I tell you something, will you promise not to laugh?" I asked him.

He shrugged and then said, "Sure."

"I saw somebody looking in the cabin window last night." I tried to say it calmly, but my heart was pounding.

"What! Who was it?" Doug asked.

"I don't know. I just saw a face. Over by that window."

We tramped over to the window. The new snow crunched under our boots. "I don't see any footprints," Doug said.

"It's been snowing all night."

My brother looked at me. "You sure you saw somebody?"

"Yes, I'm sure."

"Was it a guy?"

"Yeah."

"So how old was he? What did he look like?"

I tried to remember the face. I remembered the eyes most of all—big, dark, frightened eyes. "It looked dangerous, Doug," I said.

"Huh?" Doug stared at me.

"It did. Oh, Doug, I could feel something when it looked at me. I could feel it, like it was reaching out and touching me!"

I was trembling now just remembering the face. Nothing like this had ever happened to me before.

"You called the face 'it,' " Doug said. "I thought you said you saw a guy?"

"I did—I mean—oh, I don't know, Doug." I was sorry I'd told him anything at all. He was looking at me as if I were crazy.

"Have you told Lonnie?"

"No." I tried to smile. "Maybe I saw some animal—you know, maybe a poor old hungry bear."

"We should tell Lonnie if there are bears hanging around the cabin," Doug said.

I couldn't hide my resentment toward Lonnie. "What good would that do? Lonnie would just be scared."

A strange look came into Doug's eyes. He liked Lonnie, and it hurt him when I put Lonnie down. "Lonnie isn't a coward," he said in a cold voice.

"Okay, okay," I said. "But why should we bother him about a silly old bear?"

That wasn't really what I meant. Lonnie *was* a coward compared to my real father. Dad had flown experimental planes for the Air Force. He had been fearless. Grandmother even said Dad had been too brave for his own good. I guess maybe he was, because he was killed in a plane crash.

But I was proud of him anyway. He was a better man than Lonnie could ever be—even if Lonnie lived a hundred years.

Just then Lonnie came around the side of the cabin. He had on his green-checked lumber jacket. The jacket made him look even shorter and thinner than normal. But Lonnie always looked more like a boy than a man. Doug was almost as tall as Lonnie already.

"Tricia thinks she saw a bear last night by the window," Doug told Lonnie.

"A bear?" Lonnie whistled. "Man, oh man, let's be careful if those things are around here. Any bear out in this cold has got to be mean and hungry."

Lonnie looked alarmed, just as I had expected he would. The thought of bears scared him silly. I looked at Doug as if to say, "See, I told you so."

"I'm not real sure I saw a bear," I said.

"Well, what exactly did you see?" Lonnie asked.

"A strange face."

Lonnie laughed. He had a high-pitched laugh that really bugged me. But then everything about Lonnie bugged me.

"What kind of a face?" he asked.

"I don't know—it had large, dark, kind of angry eyes."

"Bears have little beady eyes and long snouts," Doug said. "Can't you tell the difference between a person and a bear?"

Lonnie laughed again and I felt a rush of hate for him. How nice life had been before he married Mom! He'd upset my life completely.

Worst of all was the way he'd affected Mom. Around him she acted like a sophomore in love for the first time. It was really sickening to see them together.

"Just forget it," I said, realizing there was no point in talking about it. "I was half asleep. I don't know what I saw."

"Well, it was probably a bad dream after all," Lonnie said. "I used to have a lot of bad dreams when I was a kid. I'd wake up all out of breath and frightened."

I could just imagine Lonnie having bad dreams. He was such a weak person. My dad, on the other hand, would never have admitted that he'd been upset by a dream.

I thought about the picture I had of Dad. He was standing next to his plane, a wide smile covering his face and a mischievous sparkle in his eyes. No, my dad wouldn't have been frightened of anything—especially a bad dream.

Doug seemed disappointed that what I'd seen was only part of a dream. "It would have been terrific if it had been a ghost or something."

Lonnie smiled. "Well, we can have a good time without ghosts. Can't we, Tricia?"

"Sure," I said. I would let them think it was just a bad dream. But it wasn't. If they'd seen that face in the window—

Still, it was better to let it drop. I didn't want Lonnie to get so worried he'd call Mom and spoil her visit with Aunt Sue.

Anyway, I figured I'd never see the face again. Whoever it was would never come back.

That's what I hoped anyway. I never wanted to see that ghostly face again.

2 WE DROVE TO the lodge early that evening in Lonnie's pickup truck.

"Have you ever tried to ski, Lonnie?" Doug asked.

"No. I guess I always thought I'd break a leg! I was never good at sports. I tried out for everything in school, but I never made the team."

Doug was a regular sports nut, like Dad. "You'd have made a good boxer, Lonnie. Little tough guys mix it up better than the big guys."

Lonnie laughed. "I'm little, but I'm not very tough!"

"Aw, I bet if somebody tried to shove you around, you'd give them plenty of trouble," Doug said.

"I'd try to handle it some other way," Lonnie said.

I looked out the window at the snow. I usually loved snow, but now I didn't care about it. Lonnie was like a fly in my soup.

He spoiled everything completely, even winter in the mountains.

From the first day he moved into our house, Lonnie was changing things. He even changed the way the house looked. He was an artist, so he made everything different. He got rid of our good furniture and replaced it with junk. Mom loved it, but I didn't.

He changed everything else, too. The thing I think I missed most of all was the long talks with Mom during dinner. But since Lonnie had moved in, I'd never had a chance to talk to her without Lonnie immediately jumping in.

"Here we are," Lonnie said as he pulled up to the lodge. The hearty, false tone in his voice seemed silly to me.

Inside were huge old wooden chairs, Indian rugs, and stuffed animal heads everywhere. Doug pointed to one huge buck mounted on the wall. "Hey, look! I bet they shot that around here!"

"He must have been a beautiful animal," Lonnie said. "Can you imagine how beautiful he was when he was alive?"

Doug looked sad. "Yeah."

"But somebody had to shoot him for fun," Lonnie said.

I didn't like agreeing with Lonnie about anything, but I had to agree with that. Hunting made me sad, too.

Lonnie took us up to the desk and introduced us to Rusty Dunsmuir, an old friend of his. Rusty owned Antelope Lodge. I didn't pay much attention during the introductions until I saw his son. He was a young, good-looking guy with dark brown hair.

"This is my son, Ben," Mr. Dunsmuir said.

Ben grinned at me, and we seemed to hit it off right away. He was one of those people who makes you feel good immediately. It was like we were old friends. I hoped he was the ski instructor at the lodge.

Ben soon answered my unspoken question. "I'm the guide-scout at Antelope," he explained. "Actually, I'm a jack-of-all-trades here."

Lonnie smiled. "Well, Ben, I might just

ask you to do some scouting for me. The last time I went hiking here, I got lost!"

Everybody laughed but me. Then I noticed the look that Mr. Dunsmuir and Ben exchanged. I don't think Lonnie knew it, but I could see that they were laughing at him!

While Lonnie showed Doug around the lodge, Ben and I went to the restaurant to get some hot apple cider.

"Do you like it here in the mountains?" Ben asked me as we sat down.

"I didn't want to come," I said. Usually I don't admit things like that to strangers. But Ben was so friendly. He didn't seem like a stranger.

"I can tell you're not very happy," he said.

"You can?"

"My dad knows your stepfather real well," Ben said. "I guess it must be hard getting used to a new father."

"Yeah," I said. I drank the cider slowly.

"I know something that might make your evenings more fun. Every night at eight the kids at the lodge get together for singing and dancing. I wish you'd come, too."

For the first time since I'd arrived here, I felt hopeful. "Oh, that sounds like fun!"

"I could drive you home afterward."

When we finished our drinks, I found Lonnie and asked if it would be all right if I stayed for the dance. I didn't think he had any right to boss me, but Mom thought differently. So I knew I'd better ask him.

"Oh, I was hoping you would come with Doug and me to look at the stars," was all he said. He sounded disappointed, but I didn't care.

"Yeah," Doug said, "Lonnie wants to show us Orion, the Great Hunter, through his new telescope."

I wasn't wild about Lonnie's little hobby. "Look," I said, "I'd really rather be here with Ben."

"Well, okay," Lonnie said. "But we'll miss you."

I couldn't say I'd miss him, too, so I said nothing.

I hurried back to Ben. We sat and talked

for a while. Before I knew it, I was telling him about the face at the window.

"It really frightened me, Ben."

"Sometimes strange guys hang around the cabins," Ben said. "They'll break into empty houses and steal things. Do you keep a gun?"

I laughed, "Lonnie? Keep a gun?"

Ben grinned. "He isn't exactly the hunting type, eh?"

"Hardly. He's an artist. He does pictures for kids' books!"

Ben laughed again. Then I started to tell him all the things I hated about Lonnie. I knew it wasn't right to be talking about my stepfather to a stranger. It was just that I had to tell somebody. It was all bottled up inside me.

I finally slid to an embarrassed stop and tried to dig my way out.

"Well, what do you think—about the face, I mean?" I asked.

Ben shook his head. "You better be careful if there is a prowler around the cabin," Ben said. "Could be a thief or worse."

"You know, the face looked so strange. It made me think of a poem I read once by William Blake. It was called 'Tiger' or something. I remember this one line: 'Tiger, tiger, burning bright, in the forests of the night.' For some reason that line came to me when I saw the face."

Ben looked at me, puzzled. I felt embarrassed again, so I quickly shrugged my shoulders. "Oh, well, maybe it was nothing. Maybe it was just a dream."

Around eight, Lonnie and Doug went back to the cabin. I stayed with Ben. He introduced me to all the kids. We sat around laughing and roasting marshmallows. I sort of forgot about Lonnie.

Later on, Ben and I danced. I liked that, and I was beginning to like Ben a lot, too. He seemed older than the boys at school even though he wasn't. He was seventeen, just a year older than I was.

But then, as we were dancing, he said something that sort of spoiled things.

"See the big buck near the front door?" he asked. "I shot it when I was fourteen." He seemed very proud.

"It sure is big," I said as politely as I could. But my mouth felt dry.

"Biggest one ever shot around here."

I tried not to look at the buck or remember what Lonnie had said. I told myself that there was nothing wrong with hunting. A lot of nice people hunted. Lonnie simply didn't like it because he was so timid.

I argued away my distaste. It was easy to forgive Ben for killing the buck. It's usually easy to forgive people you like.

"You must be a very good shot," I told Ben. He smiled; I'd made him happy. The only thing was, I wasn't being truthful and I didn't feel right about that. But I was having so much fun with Ben, I didn't care.

After all, it was just a buck. He was probably old. He would have died soon anyway. I felt sure that Ben's shot had been quick and clean.

Around ten, Ben drove me back to the cabin. I hated to see the evening end.

Ben pulled up to the cabin and stopped. "The cabin looks dark," he commented.

"Are you sure your stepfather and brother are home?"

"Lonnie must still be stargazing," I said. "He goes up that hill over there. He loses all track of time when he's looking at the stars."

Ben laughed. "Do you think your stepfather is making your brother into a stargazer, too?"

I'd never thought of it like that before. Now I felt angry. Lonnie had no right to spoil Doug! Just because he was weak, it didn't give him the right to spoil Doug. Doug should grow up to be like Dad!

"I hope not," I said.

"Yeah," Ben agreed. "It would be a shame if Doug turned out strange."

I looked at Ben. "Could you maybe teach Doug to ski or something? I hate to think of him spending all his time with Lonnie!"

"Sure. I could teach him to shoot, too. I started hunting when I was twelve."

"I don't think Lonnie would like him to handle guns."

"But your brother has the right to learn

if he wants to."

The truth was, I didn't want Doug to learn to shoot, either. I'd seen kids in our neighborhood shooting birds. It had made me sick. But I didn't tell Ben that. Instead I just said, "Maybe you could stick with the skiing, huh, Ben?"

"Sure. It's just that I have so much fun hunting. Well, we'll start with skiing lessons if you want." He looked at the dark cabin. "Can you get in okay, Tricia?"

"Oh, sure. I have a key. Thanks for driving me home, Ben."

I waved as he drove off. I was sorry to see him go.

As I walked to the door, I glanced up at the sky. The moon hung there like a curved icicle among a crowd of stars. Lonnie had picked a good night for his stargazing.

I stuck my key in the door and went inside. It was a little chilly indoors, so I checked the woodpile. We were almost out of wood. I figured I'd get some wood off the pile outdoors while I waited for Doug and Lonnie to return.

I went out to the woodpile and started gathering logs. Suddenly I felt funny. I got this queasy feeling in my stomach. I felt as though something was watching me.

I turned around slowly and peered into the darkness. Nothing. I sighed with relief. Then I scolded myself for letting my imagination get the better of me. "Tricia, you idiot," I muttered, "stop acting like a scared little kid!"

I picked up enough wood for a good fire and started back to the cabin.

Then I saw him. There could be no doubt this time. I wasn't dreaming; he was real.

He didn't move; he just stood there watching me. I began to shake. The wood tumbled to the ground. My arms and legs were numb.

I wanted to run but I couldn't. I read once that a bird will not fly away when it sees a snake. It simply cannot.

I felt like that. I couldn't move. I simply stared as the ghostly figure moved closer.

3 IN THE WEAK light of the moon, I saw the same dark eyes I'd seen before. Now they were wet, as if he were crying. Slowly, I made out the rest of him. He was small and thin, sort of like Lonnie. Shiny black hair fell in a tangle around his shoulders. He wore a ragged shirt and pants—and only a thin jacket.

He was crouching, making himself even smaller. He held out his hands as if he were asking for something.

"Who are you?" I asked him. My own voice frightened me. I scarcely recognized it as mine.

The look in his eyes never changed. The night was so still that I could hear him breathing. He was panting, as though he couldn't get enough air.

He was between me and the cabin. I had to get by him, but I was afraid to make a quick move. I took one small step, and he leaped a little. He jumped like a rabbit, animal-like.

His mouth was open, but he didn't say anything. I don't know why, but that frightened me more than anything. It was as though he was as scared as I was.

Suddenly, in the distance, I heard Doug singing. I turned and looked in that direction. I wanted to scream for help, but I couldn't make a sound.

Then I heard a crashing sound in the brush. I turned and saw the ghostly figure was gone. I figured that Doug's singing had scared him away.

I sank to the ground, weak and numb. In a few minutes, Doug appeared in the clearing. When he spotted me, he stopped and stared.

"Tricia!" he exclaimed. "You look like you've just seen a ghost!"

I couldn't answer him. "What's the matter?" he asked. "What happened?"

"I saw him again," I whispered. "He was here, right here!"

Then Lonnie appeared. He looked from one to the other of us and then asked, "What's the matter?"

"It was him—the face at the window. I

saw him again!" I stammered.

I shook with fright at the memory. I remembered his huge eyes and the way he looked at me with his mouth open. But mostly I remembered that line from Blake's poem:

Tiger, tiger, burning bright . . .

Lonnie reached out and tried to put his arm around me. I guess he wanted to comfort me. But I moved away. He looked very hurt, but I didn't want him to touch me.

"Come on inside the cabin," he said. I didn't need to be urged a second time.

Inside, Lonnie quickly made some hot chocolate, and we sat around the table to drink it. Then Lonnie said, "Tell me exactly what happened."

"Ben dropped me off. When I came inside, I saw we were low on wood. So I went outside to get some. When I turned around, he was in the clearing."

"What did he really look like, Trish?" Doug asked eagerly. He was more excited than frightened by my experience. The idea of a mysterious stranger lurking in the woods appealed to him. Like Dad, he was too brave for his own good.

"He had wild, black hair and dark, staring eyes. As big as an owl's."

"Wow!" Doug said.

Lonnie suddenly spoke up. "Why do you talk about him as though he were an animal?"

I looked at Lonnie. "Well, he sure wasn't like any person I've ever seen."

"Tricia, are you sure your imagination isn't adding a little bit to this?" Lonnie asked me. He didn't want to believe my story. I didn't either. But it was true. Some man or boy was hiding out there.

"I know what I saw. He stared at me and he moved like an animal—like a rabbit."

Lonnie gazed at me for a minute. Then he said, "Drink your hot chocolate. You'll feel better." He got up and began putting on his coat.

"What are you going to do?" I asked.

"Just look around a little bit."

"And what will you do if you see him?

He might be dangerous. You can't just throw a stick at him." I guess I sounded nasty. I was implying that Lonnie couldn't handle himself well.

He spoke calmly. "Look, Tricia, this person you saw could be a lost child or a runaway. If that's the case, he probably needs help."

"That wasn't a little kid I saw!"

"You said it might have been a boy."

"I said it was small like a boy, but he—he's not a child."

"Maybe it's something—well, supernatural," Doug said.

Lonnie shook his head. "I've never believed in ghosts. And since I'm almost forty years old, I'm too old to start believing now."

"Well, I felt something," I said. "Some power. Like he was reaching out to me."

"Maybe he *was*. Maybe he was asking for help," Lonnie said.

"I still think it's dangerous. I don't think you should go out there," I said.

Lonnie went outside anyway. As the door closed behind him, Doug looked at me proudly. "See. He's no coward," he declared.

"He's stupid!" I snapped.

I knew Lonnie wouldn't find anything. I just had the feeling that the ghost wouldn't show himself to Lonnie. And I knew Lonnie wouldn't find footprints either. I was right.

"I didn't see anything," Lonnie said when he came back inside. He stamped the snow from his boots, then walked over to the fireplace to warm himself.

"Did you look in the snow for footprints?" I asked him.

"I looked all over. I didn't see anything." He poured himself some hot chocolate. "It's cold out there, really cold."

"I guess you don't believe that I saw anything," I said.

Lonnie put his cup down. "I didn't say that, Tricia. I'm sure you really did see something. But for now, I'm going to let it rest. In the morning I'll go out and look some more."

About an hour later, we all went to bed. But I couldn't sleep. I just lay there staring at the cabin window. I wondered if the face would be there again tonight. Maybe if I closed my eyes, I could keep it from coming. But I couldn't close them.

I guess I went to sleep then because I began to dream. It was a strange, terrible dream. I saw the face again, and it had the same intense eyes. But this time it got very close, and I knew whose face I was seeing. It was *Lonnie's* face!

I gasped in terror and woke up. Sweat covered my body. I didn't fall asleep until sunup.

After breakfast we went down to the lodge. Lonnie told Mr. Dunsmuir, "Tricia thinks we might have a prowler at the cabin."

Mr. Dunsmuir looked at me. "Things missing?"

"No, but I saw somebody."

Ben came up then. "So you saw him again, Tricia?"

"Yes. This time he was in the clearing by the woodpile."

"I don't like the sound of this," Mr. Dunsmuir said. "Tricia's prowler could be dangerous or crazy. You people might be in danger."

Lonnie smiled. "I don't think so. I think our visitor is just a runaway kid."

"Ben and I could come and take a look," Mr. Dunsmuir said. "We'll break out a couple of rifles and—"

"I don't think so, Rusty," Lonnie said. "Thanks just the same."

Ben winked at me, sharing our private joke. I had told him that Lonnie didn't like guns—that he was a coward. Now I was sort of sorry I had mentioned it.

"Mr. Boone," Ben said, "don't you think it would be safer if Dad and I took a quick check around?"

Lonnie smiled at Ben. "No need to bother. I'll just tell Sheriff Somers and let him look around."

"Sheriff Somers will take a month to get to it," Mr. Dunsmuir grumbled. "Better let us handle it."

"I said, no thank you." Lonnie's voice was hard. He and Rusty Dunsmuir stared at each other for what seemed like a long time.

Suddenly I saw that the two men really didn't like each other much. I hadn't noticed that before. I knew they had known each other a long time. I'd just assumed they were friends.

Mr. Dunsmuir finally muttered, "Suit yourself." He turned and strode away, Ben at his heels.

I asked Lonnie, "Why didn't you let them look around? I thought it was a good idea."

"I don't want trouble. People running around with rifles can end up hurting someone."

"But what about the prowler?" Doug asked.

"I said I'd call the sheriff."

"I don't think you care if we catch the prowler or not," I said.

Lonnie seemed about to answer me, but he stopped. He turned and asked Doug to go buy a newspaper. Then when Doug was out of earshot, he asked, "Tricia, why did you say that? Do you really believe I don't care about the prowler?"

"I don't know." I couldn't get that crazy

dream out of my head. I kept seeing the ghost boy's face turn into Lonnie's face. It gave me a funny feeling. Especially now that it seemed Lonnie wasn't very eager to investigate.

"Tricia, I wonder if you know how people like Mr. Dunsmuir really are," Lonnie said.

"That's a strange thing to say. What do you mean?"

Lonnie's eyes turned dark. "Violent people who let their emotions get the better of them."

"What do you mean? Maybe Mr. Dunsmuir isn't the kind of person you are, so you don't understand him. But I do. He's like my dad was."

Lonnie looked hurt. He said, "You don't think very highly of me, do you?"

"I never said that," I protested.

"But you think it," Lonnie replied.

All of a sudden, I realized that Lonnie knew I didn't like him. I felt strange. I'd never thought he knew how much I disliked him.

"You think a real man loves sports and hunts and wears a dozen war medals," he continued. He seemed mad, and it frightened me.

"Stop putting words into my mouth," I objected. But my voice was shaking.

"You don't like me, Tricia, do you?" he insisted.

I wanted desperately to get away from him. I'd never seen Lonnie so upset. And as I stared into his eyes, he seemed to change. I saw something wild there—as wild as the ghost boy's haunted eyes.

4 I COULDN'T SAY anything for a moment. At last I blurted out, "You're talking nonsense." Then I turned and hurried away.

I looked for Ben. He wasn't anywhere in the lodge, so I went outside.

I found him with Doug on the ski slopes. It seemed Ben and Doug had hit it off really well. Doug had fallen off his skis and looked like a huge snowball. But he was laughing.

When Doug saw me, he took off his skis and came toward me. "Hi, Tricia. Boy, you should try this. It's great!"

I smiled, though the corners of my mouth trembled. "Maybe I will."

"That'd be great," Ben seconded. "Hey, I've got to go check in with my dad about the schedule for next week. Come see me up at the lodge, Trish, in about ten minutes. And you, Doug, keep practicing." He waved and quickly set off for the lodge.

Doug stared in admiration after Ben for a moment. Then he announced, "Ben wants to teach me to shoot."

"Lonnie wouldn't like that," I warned.

"But why? Ben's a real good teacher. He'd make sure everything was safe."

"You know how Lonnie feels about dangerous things, especially guns," I said.

Doug gave me a dirty look. "You're saying he's a coward again, aren't you? Well, that shows how much you know. Last night he climbed way to the top of the mountain. It was all ice and rocks— really dangerous. He climbed so high, I couldn't even see him anymore."

"Really? I thought you and Lonnie were together the whole time."

"No. He was gone for a pretty long while."

An unpleasant thought came to me. If Lonnie hadn't been with Doug, maybe he'd doubled back to the cabin. Maybe the strange person in the clearing had been Lonnie.

Then I started thinking about the first time I'd seen the face. It was only *after* the face had disappeared that I actually saw Lonnie standing in the room. I hadn't seen both of them at exactly the same time.

What if Lonnie were the ghost boy? Suppose he had a split personality, a secret side? Like Dr. Jekyll and Mr. Hyde.

"Tricia, you look funny. What's the matter?" Doug asked.

"Nothing."

"Are you mad at Lonnie or something?"

"Of course not," I said. I wasn't mad anymore—I was frightened.

Just then I spotted Lonnie making his way down the slope toward us. He had a big smile for Doug.

"How'd your skiing go?" he called. "Did you have a good time?"

"Yeah, I sure did. I fell down a million times, but it was fun."

Then Lonnie looked at me and his smile disappeared. "I called the sheriff. He's coming out to the cabin when he has time."

"Good," I said. I tried to avoid looking at Lonnie, but I couldn't help it. I stared into his eyes. Before, they'd always seemed like plain old dark eyes. Now they looked bright—and scary. I began to shake again, and I turned away.

"Is something wrong?" Lonnie asked me.

"No—no. I'm just a little cold. I think I'll go back to the lodge now. Don't worry about me; Ben will drive me home."

I found Ben, and we went to his room to listen to records. I was glad for the chance to be alone with him. After we'd talked for about an hour, he said he'd drive me to the cabin.

On the ride back, Ben laughed and said, "Your stepfather sure is chicken. He looked like he was going to faint when Dad mentioned rifles!"

"I guess he's afraid somebody will get hurt," I said. I wanted to tell Ben about my fears, but I couldn't. Even he would laugh at me. Lonnie turning into someone different by the light of the moon! It was like something from a horror movie.

Maybe it was all my imagination, I thought. I disliked Lonnie so much that my mind was playing tricks on me.

I tried to put Lonnie out of my mind. "Doug seems to like you a lot, Ben," I said.

"He's a great kid. He's got guts."

"He's like our dad."

"He wants to learn to shoot," Ben said.

"I know. He told me."

When we got to the cabin, Ben said, "Would you mind if I looked around here on my own? I could come by this afternoon. No need to tell anybody."

I smiled. "I'd like that, Ben."

"Good," he said. Then he looked very serious. "Tricia, did your mom date Lonnie for a long time before they were married?"

It seemed a funny question for Ben to ask, but I answered anyway. "No," I said, "they got married pretty quick. They met when Mom took a ceramics class—he was the teacher. About eight months after they'd met, they decided to get married. Why do you ask?"

"I just wondered how well you knew him."

"Is there something wrong, Ben?" I was feeling nervous again.

Ben hesitated. I could see he had

something on his mind but didn't want to say it. He finally sighed and said, "Dad has known Lonnie a long time—they were kids together. Well, last night Dad told me something about Lonnie. I was really shocked. I think you should know about it."

"What is it, Ben?" By now my nerves were raw.

"Your stepfather—he's had a history of mental illness," Ben said.

I stared at Ben. The words "mental illness" stunned me. A picture of wild, raving people came to my mind.

I felt scared and a little ashamed at the same time. I knew that mental illness was just another kind of illness. But the fear kept bubbling up inside me.

"How sick was he, Ben?"

"He was in a hospital for a long time."

"When?"

"Well, I guess when he was a kid. Maybe I shouldn't have mentioned it. I didn't mean to scare you."

"I'm okay," I said. I got out of the truck.

"I'll look around this afternoon. Okay, Trish?"

"Sure, okay, Ben."

I walked toward the cabin and nervously went inside. Nobody was home, so I just sat on my cot and thought about Lonnie.

I remembered the first time Mom had brought him home. That time, I had thought he was okay.

Then he started to come to the house almost every night. It was like Mom didn't see Doug and me anymore. Lonnie was the star of the show. Mom would laugh at him and talk about the stupid things he was interested in.

At that point I really started to dislike Lonnie. So when Mom said she was going to marry him, I was sick.

Now I wondered if she had known Lonnie's history. Would she have married him if she'd known he'd been in a mental hospital?

Early in the afternoon, Doug and Lonnie came home. They were laughing together, just like a real father and son.

"We got some hot dogs and marsh-mallows," Doug said when they came inside. He dropped a big grocery bag on the table.

"Maybe Tricia can stay home with us tonight," Lonnie said. "Maybe she won't go to the lodge." He was smiling, but he sounded a little irritated.

"I planned on staying home," I said.

"Good," Lonnie said. "It should be a pretty evening. In fact, I think I'll paint tonight. I'll paint moonlight on the snow."

"Yeah?" Doug grinned.

"I'll take my canvas outside and paint the moon when it rises."

"Won't you freeze out there?" I asked him.

"No, I'll wear my lumber jacket," he said.

He went outside at eight. Doug and I were still roasting marshmallows. Doug was telling me about his skiing. I tried to act interested, but all I could think of was what Ben had said.

By nine, I started to wonder what had happened to Lonnie when he still hadn't come in.

"He must be turning into a snowman," I said.

"Yeah," Doug said. "I'm going out there and tell him to come inside."

Doug and I put on our leather jackets and went outside. Doug carried a big flashlight.

"Look, there's his canvas," he said. "But I don't see Lonnie."

I explored the clearing while Doug scouted around the cabin. I heard him shouting, "Lonnie isn't back here!"

Lonnie's picture caught my eye. I walked over to the canvas. When I saw what he had painted, I gasped. On the canvas was the face I had seen in the window and again in the clearing!

There could be no mistake. The face had the same dark eyes, hair, and skin.

I heard Doug come up behind me. "Hey, Tricia—" he began.

Then he caught sight of the picture, too. "Wow!" he said. He turned to me. "Who *is* that, Trish?"

"It's—the face I saw," I said.

"That means Lonnie saw it, too. He must have been painting and he saw the boy. And he painted him!" Doug looked frightened. "Tricia, maybe Lonnie was attacked. I mean, where is he? Where's Lonnie?"

"He's—he's probably just taking a walk," I said. I tried to sound calm.

"Maybe he was dragged into the woods," Doug said. "We have to find him! He might be hurt!"

At that moment a long, drawn-out cry pierced the night. I wanted to scream, but my throat closed up.

I grabbed Doug's arm. "Come on! We have to get inside the cabin!"

Doug wouldn't budge. "What was it?" he whispered. His eyes swallowed his face.

"Just a wolf," I said. "Must be a wolf."

"That didn't sound like a wolf to me. Maybe—maybe it was Lonnie—"

"Oh, Doug, don't be silly. But we shouldn't be outside. It's too cold."

My heart was pounding and I could hardly breathe. I pushed Doug into the cabin, then closed the door and bolted it shut.

"Trish, we have to go out and find Lonnie!" Doug yelled.

"I know he's all right," I lied. I couldn't help thinking that Doug was right. Maybe Lonnie had been attacked. Maybe he was out there right now, hurt.

"Come on! Why would he just leave his painting there? He must be in trouble. I bet something happened to him."

We heard footsteps then. The snow was deep and the sounds were heavy.

I ran to the window, half fearing what I would see. At first I couldn't spot anything. It was snowing hard, and the flakes were like a thick curtain.

But then I saw a figure. Somebody was coming—somebody small and thin. I saw the figure near the cabin, bent against the wind.

"Is that Lonnie coming? Do you see him?" Doug asked anxiously.

I felt sick and frightened. My mouth was as dry as chalk. "I see somebody," I said.

"Is it Lonnie?" Doug asked again.

I didn't know who that figure in the snow was. I didn't even know who Lonnie was. But how could I tell Doug that? How could I tell him about my wild fears?

I kept thinking about what Ben had said. Maybe Lonnie *was* the person I had seen in the window. Maybe he changed personality—became a wild man—and didn't even know about it.

I backed away from the window, breathing like I'd run a mile. Did I dare unlock the door?

I saw the knob jiggle. Then someone pounded on the door. Whoever was out there wanted in—now.

5 "LET ME IN! Hey!" It was Lonnie's voice. I pushed back the bolt and he came in. The canvas was tucked under his arm.

"I'm afraid I cheated on my work," he explained as he took off his coat. "I didn't paint after all. I looked at the stars instead."

"Lonnie," I said, gazing right into his eyes, "I saw the painting."

He put the canvas down on the table. "Oh, I did a few clouds, that's all."

I examined the canvas. The face was gone; he had painted over it.

"You painted the face out."

"What are you talking about?" He stared at us with wary eyes, like a trapped animal. Then he seemed to understand that we'd both seen the painting.

He smiled a funny smile. "I was trying to do a modern painting. It didn't turn out, so I painted over it."

"Lonnie, you painted the face Tricia

saw," Doug said.

"Did I? I didn't mean to. I guess I was thinking about it and I painted it."

Doug said, "We thought maybe you saw someone out there."

"No, I didn't. All I saw were stars, snow, and trees."

I knew he was lying. But we went to bed without saying any more about it.

I lay awake for a long time. And then, at about eleven, I saw Lonnie get out of his sleeping bag. He got up very slowly. He was being careful not to wake us. He didn't know I was already awake.

The moon was shining through the window, so I could see Lonnie clearly. He walked over to the sink and rolled up his sleeve.

I had to cover my mouth with my hand to stop from crying out. Lonnie had blood all over his arm!

He washed and washed until the blood was gone. Then he wrapped a bandage around his arm. When he finished, he went back to his sleeping bag.

I lay there shaking, wondering what to

believe. I felt certain he'd seen the strange boy. How else could he have painted such a close copy of his face? So why had he lied about it?

I knew something else, too. Something violent had happened out there tonight.

In spite of all my worry, I did fall asleep. When I woke up, it was morning. The rich smell of buttermilk pancakes hung in the air.

I sat up and stared cautiously at Lonnie. He was busy in the kitchen whipping up the pancakes.

He caught sight of me and called out cheerfully, "Good morning."

I looked at Doug's cot. It was empty. "Where's Doug?"

"Outside getting some firewood," Lonnie said.

I slipped into a robe. "Need any help with breakfast?"

"No."

I thought about the blood on his arm last night. Almost without thinking about it, I said, "How did you hurt yourself, Lonnie?"

He almost dropped the bowl of pancake mix. That same trapped look came over his face.

"What do you mean?" he asked.

"Last night. I saw you cleaning the blood off your arm. It looked like a pretty bad wound to me."

"Oh, I just slipped on a rock. It's nothing."

"Maybe you should get a tetanus shot," I said.

"It's nice of you to be concerned. But it's okay." He tried to smile. "I had a tetanus shot a year ago."

It wasn't just a small wound—it was a bad gash. But I knew it was useless to ask him any more. He would just lie about it.

I thought about Mom in Philadelphia. How I wished I were with her. We were supposed to call her today from the lodge. I longed to tell her how I felt.

Yet at the same time, I didn't want to worry her. I still wasn't sure anything was *really* wrong. But I didn't trust Lonnie, and I hated to think of spending two weeks with him.

"Sheriff is coming over this morning to look around," Lonnie said as he poured maple syrup on our pancakes.

"Is he?" I guess I sounded surprised.

"I told you I called him," Lonnie said.

I felt better. If Lonnie had called the sheriff, maybe he didn't have something to hide after all. I even smiled and said, "These are good pancakes."

Lonnie said "Thanks," but he didn't smile. I guess things were spoiled between us. He knew how I felt.

Maybe it could have been different. Maybe when Lonnie first came to our house I could have been nicer. I could have opened my heart a crack.

But he'd changed my life—our lives—so much. He'd assumed he could just walk in and take Dad's place. I wasn't ready for that. I couldn't imagine I would ever be. It was too late now anyway.

The sheriff came over about ten that morning. Lonnie asked him in for coffee. I could see they were old friends.

When Lonnie introduced me, the sheriff smiled and said, "I understand you saw a prowler, young lady."

I felt silly. He was treating me like a foolish little kid with a big imagination.

"Yes, I saw something."

"Something? Just what did you see?"

"A face—a strange-looking face."

Lonnie smiled at the sheriff. I could see it all very clearly now. He was encouraging the sheriff to think I was imagining things.

The sheriff grinned back. "Maybe she saw Bigfoot, eh?" he joked. They both laughed.

Sheriff Somers did walk around the cabin a few times. However, he didn't seem to be looking for anything. He just seemed to be doing his duty. He wrote some things in his little notebook and then said to Lonnie, "Well, if anything else happens, be sure to let me know."

"Sure," Lonnie said, "and thanks for coming. I'm sorry we brought you out here for nothing."

"That's what I'm here for," the sheriff said, "to check out things for folks." He turned to me. "Don't you worry, young lady. What you saw was probably just a kid with a Halloween mask. Just some kid playing a prank. Likely you won't be bothered again." With that, he walked to his car and drove away.

I turned to Lonnie. "Well, he sure thinks I'm a fool."

"No, he doesn't."

"You know him from way back, don't you?"

"Yeah, I do. You know I've had this cabin a long time. I grew up around here." His voice trailed off. Then he seemed to return to the present. "Well, maybe it's best if we just forget the whole thing, Tricia," he said.

"Forget it?" I was angry again. "But I saw him!"

"I bet it's just what Charlie said: a kid playing a joke."

There was no use talking about it. I turned away and looked at the glistening white mountain. "Okay, we'll just forget about it."

"Good girl," he said. But he didn't soothe my anger.

We spent the morning around the cabin. Then early that afternoon, we all three drove to the lodge.

As we pulled up to the lodge, Lonnie said, "Let's not mention anything about the prowler to your mom. No need to worry her."

"Sure," Doug said.

"Yeah," I agreed. What else could I say?

So when we called Mom, we told her everything was okay.

"I miss you, Mom," I said.

"I miss you too, darling," Mom said. "Love and kisses to everybody."

Lonnie talked to her then. I walked away. I couldn't stand to listen to another one of their personal conversations.

I found Ben and we went for a walk outside. I told him about the painting Lonnie had done.

"That sure proves your stepfather knows more than he's saying," Ben said.

"Did you have a chance to look around the cabin yesterday?" I asked him.

"Yeah. I didn't come across anything— not even footprints. That prowler of yours is probably hiding in a cave somewhere. There are a lot of caves around here."

Ben looked very serious. "I did find a pretty big cave about a mile from your place. There were a bunch of bones scattered around. Seemed like an animal lived there."

"That boy I saw, he sure acts like an animal," I said with a shudder.

"Yeah?"

I paused and then asked what had been weighing on my mind. "Ben, you know what you said yesterday? About your dad and Lonnie being kids together?"

"Yeah."

"Do you think I could talk to your dad sometime?" I felt funny making the suggestion. Talking about Lonnie behind his back made me uneasy. But I just had to know the truth about him.

"Sure. In fact, he's not busy now. Come on. He's right in the den."

I followed Ben into the huge den. His father was at the desk.

Ben explained to his father why I had come. Mr. Dunsmuir smiled at me. "Sit down, Tricia. Well, what do you want to know?"

"I just wondered if you could tell me about Lonnie being a kid. I—I want to understand him better."

Mr. Dunsmuir leaned back in his leather chair. "I don't think any of us really knew Lonnie as a boy. He was a loner."

Like "mental illness," the word "loner" brought bad images to mind. It seemed that whenever a crime was committed, a "loner" had done it.

"I remember a bunch of us kids were always playing games together," Mr. Dunsmuir said. "Not Lonnie. He'd just slip off by himself and disappear for a long time. I think sometimes he'd climb a tree and just sit there."

"Maybe he was painting pictures," I said.

"Yes. He'd do that sometimes. But other times he'd just sit and stare."

Mr. Dunsmuir paused and looked at me. "And then he had the mental breakdown. Do you want to know about that, Tricia?" His voice was very soft.

"Yes," I said.

"He was about ten. One day he went off by himself. We followed him. A bunch of us kids followed him. We found him in a clearing, making these funny noises. Well, the kids all laughed. And he went sort of crazy, Tricia."

"What do you mean?"

"He came at us like a wild animal. He got a big rock and started beating on us. Then he attacked Billy. Poor Billy. He was laughing a lot, and that made Lonnie mad. He really went at Billy—"

"And then what?"

"They had to put Lonnie away. He was in a hospital for a year."

His words just hung there. I kept hearing them over and over: *They had to put Lonnie away.*

6 "TRICIA, I DON'T want to upset you," Mr. Dunsmuir said. "But I'm uneasy about you kids being alone with him out there. I'll be honest with you. I don't trust Lonnie; I've never trusted him. He's strange and always has been."

I remembered what Lonnie had said about Mr. Dunsmuir: *Violent people who let their emotions get the better of them.* I didn't know whom to believe.

"Mr. Dunsmuir, Lonnie doesn't seem dangerous," I said.

"Well, you never know about a man like that. I just think you ought to live here at the lodge. We have plenty of room. You and Doug could stay here. You could see Ben every day. I bet Ben would like the idea." He smiled. "Isn't that so?"

Ben grinned. "You bet."

I smiled at both of them. "It's very kind of you. But it would be like telling Lonnie I don't trust him. He would be hurt. And then he'd tell Mom, and she'd be hurt. I'm not sure how I feel about Lonnie, but I do care about my mom's feelings."

Mr. Dunsmuir looked very serious. "But I think your safety is more important than anybody's feelings."

I knew Mr. Dunsmuir meant well. But I just couldn't do it. Mom would never forgive me. Besides, I couldn't actually imagine Lonnie hurting Doug or me. So I thanked Mr. Dunsmuir and went with Ben.

We slowly walked outside together, not saying much. We finally ended up at Inspiration Point.

We stood at the guardrail and looked into the valley. It was a beautiful sight. Sugary snow clung to the pines. The whole valley glittered like a Christmas card.

"It must be wonderful to live here all the time," I said.

"It is. But the long bus trip to school is a drag," Ben said.

"Are you a senior now?"

"Yeah. I'll be graduating this June."

"I wish I were," I said. "I wish I were totally finished with high school."

Ben smiled. "Don't you like high school?"

"Oh, it's okay. As a matter of fact, I've always liked school. But now I want to go away to college."

Ben nodded. "No good at home, huh?"

"It used to be great. I used to think I'd live at home and go to City College. I always got along so well with Mom. Doug and I always got along, too. I used to think how lucky I was."

"Too bad she married that guy," Ben said.

"Well, Mom's happy," I had to admit.

Ben laughed. "I wonder what she sees in him."

That sort of made me feel bad. I sure didn't like Lonnie myself. Yet it didn't seem like Ben had any right to talk that way about my family.

"Well, I guess he has his good points. It's just that I don't like him."

"Let's not waste time talking about him," Ben smiled. "Here I am at Inspiration Point with a beautiful girl. I should be thinking of you."

I smiled. "I'm sure you take a lot of girls here." He was handsome. I figured he had a lot of girl friends.

"No, no, I don't. You're special, Tricia." He slipped his arm around my shoulders. I didn't mind.

We stood quietly for a moment. Then he pointed to some skiers off in the distance. "You should let me teach you to ski, Tricia," he urged.

"I'd like that."

"Good. We'll plan on it. You know, Tricia, it would be great if you lived at the lodge. Are you sure you don't want to? It would make me feel a lot better."

"I'd like to, but I can't."

Ben shook his head. "I can't help worrying about you out there in that lonely cabin with your stepfather."

"Oh, Ben, I don't like him, but he's harmless."

"But you heard what Dad said," Ben insisted.

"Yeah. But little kids fight all the time. That happened a long time ago."

"Tricia, just the same, Bill Ebbetson

died," Ben said.

For a moment I couldn't believe what I'd just heard. The whole white mountain blurred before my eyes.

I turned. "Ben, what are you talking about?"

"Dad told you, didn't he?" Ben looked funny.

Then I remembered Ben had left during part of the conversation I had with his father. He'd thought his father had told me more than he did.

"Ben, your dad said Lonnie attacked Billy. I just thought they had a fight—"

Ben hung his head. "Me and my big mouth. I'm sorry, Tricia. I don't want to frighten you."

I was desperate. "Ben, tell me what happened!"

"Well, Lonnie attacked Billy—I don't know how. My dad didn't see just what happened. There were about eight kids. Everybody was shouting and screaming. But Dad said Lonnie had a rock, and Bill got his head bashed in."

My legs went numb. I wondered why I

was still standing.

"Are you telling me that Lonnie killed that other boy?"

"I'm sorry, Tricia. I shouldn't have said anything. They were kids. Like you said, it was a long time ago. It wasn't Lonnie's fault. He was sick. He had to be put in a hospital, you know."

I stumbled back down the trail. Ben hurriedly followed and caught up with me. "I'm really sorry," he said again.

"I'm going to ask Lonnie what happened," I said. "I have to know the truth."

"Tricia, you better not ask him. He might get real upset."

I turned to Ben, almost in anger. "You mean he might go crazy, don't you? That's what you mean!"

"Trish, please. I'm sorry."

We walked back to the lodge in silence. I knew I couldn't ask Lonnie. He'd discover that I'd been prying into his past. He might get angry and lose his temper like he had before.

When I got to the lodge, I tried not to act differently with Lonnie. But he seemed to sense something was wrong. He kept looking at me suspiciously. I thought maybe he didn't like me going away and not telling him what I was doing.

"It's time we got back to the cabin," he told me sharply. Then he asked, "Where's Doug?"

"I thought he was with you," I told him.

"Well, he must be around somewhere."

We looked in the lobby of the lodge, but Doug wasn't there. Just then we spotted Mr. Dunsmuir. Lonnie approached him and asked, "Have you seen Doug?"

"Sure. I saw him a little while ago. I loaned him a pair of old skis. He thought it might be fun to ski back to the cabin."

"Shouldn't you have asked me first?" Lonnie almost shouted.

Mr. Dunsmuir looked surprised. "Well, Lonnie, it's just a short distance. The boy told me he was getting to be pretty good with skis."

"Pretty good! He's only been at it for a few days! What if he falls somewhere and breaks his leg? He could freeze to death out there while we searched for him!"

Lonnie's voice was loud and furious. I'd never seen him so angry.

"Oh, come on, Lonnie," Mr. Dunsmuir said with disgust. "The boy is twelve years old. Old enough to spread his wings a little, don't you think?"

"I think it's none of your business!" Lonnie shouted. "I'll thank you to mind your own business where my family is concerned!"

Mr. Dunsmuir caught my eye and shook his head sadly. But I didn't have time to say even a word to him. Lonnie was rushing out of the lodge; I had to run to keep up with him. His face was strained and he was shaking.

Frankly, I couldn't see what he was so upset about. It didn't seem very likely that Doug would break his leg. And he did seem to be learning how to ski pretty fast.

I tried to reassure Lonnie. "Doug is usually really careful," I said.

"It doesn't seem particularly careful for a beginning skier to head out in the wilderness by himself," Lonnie snapped.

We got into the pickup truck and

headed down the road. Though I hoped we might see Doug skiing near the road-side, we didn't. But then I thought he had probably reached home already.

However, Doug wasn't at the cabin when we got there. I didn't see the skis either.

"Where is he?" Lonnie muttered.

"He must have gone exploring," I said.

"Oh, that's great!" he snapped. He was breathing very hard. He stalked around the cabin and even peered into the tool shed. "I thought Doug was more respon-sible than this! Man, when I find that kid!"

I began to be frightened again. I thought Lonnie might hurt Doug when he found him.

"Doug didn't mean any harm," I said. "He's just a kid."

"He should have asked me if he could ski home!"

"He just wasn't thinking! And don't you dare hurt him when you find him!" I didn't mean to yell, but I did.

Lonnie turned and looked at me. "What did you say?"

"You heard me, all right!"

"Yes, I did. And how I deal with that boy is up to me. He's my responsibility now." He sounded bitter.

"You're not his father!" I shouted at him.

"Don't you tell me what I am!" He was so angry that I didn't dare say another word. I just followed him as he went out to search for Doug.

Lonnie immediately set off into the woods. I had to run to keep up. He kept looking at the ground. I guess he was looking for ski tracks.

Suddenly he stopped. I saw it, too. A skier had come this way, all right.

The sky was turning dark. Huge snow clouds were gathering, and I knew it would be snowing hard soon.

I began to worry about Doug, too. It got very cold up here. Doug was not even dressed warmly.

Why hadn't he come home yet? He must see that it was getting dark. He knew what it was like here when it snowed. Had something bad happened to him?

What if he'd fallen and hurt himself?

What if he were unconscious somewhere? What if a wild animal had attacked him?

My heart began to pound in my chest. I looked at Lonnie. His mouth was a hard line in his grim face.

7 WE BOTH HEARD Doug's voice at the same moment. He was shouting from somewhere, but the wind was so strong that we had trouble telling where he was.

Finally we found him in a small ravine. He wasn't hurt, but he couldn't get out.

Lonnie crouched at the edge of the ravine. "You okay?"

"Yeah. I skidded on some ice." Doug smiled. "I sure am glad to see you. I took off the skis, but I can't seem to climb out of here."

Lonnie took off his belt and held it down to Doug. Very slowly Doug climbed up the rocks, Lonnie giving directions and sometimes pulling him.

When Doug was safely out, Lonnie said in a sharp voice, "Why did you go off without telling me?"

Doug seemed surprised by Lonnie's anger. "I'm sorry. I guess I got so excited about skiing that I just forgot."

"Well, don't you ever forget a thing like that again!" Lonnie barked at him.

"Sure, I won't. I'm sorry." Doug looked back into the ravine at the skis. "I'll have to get those out of there somehow and back to Mr. Dunsmuir."

"Leave them there," Lonnie said.

"But they belong to Mr. Dunsmuir. He loaned them to me. If we leave them here, they'll get ruined."

"I said to leave them," Lonnie shouted. He grabbed Doug's arm. "Come on. We have a long, cold walk home."

We walked back to the cabin in total silence. Lonnie was still angry, and Doug looked hurt and mixed-up. I wondered what Doug thought of Lonnie now. Doug had never seen Lonnie like this before.

When we reached the cabin, Lonnie made hot chocolate. "Drink plenty of it. You almost froze out there, Doug," Lonnie said. His voice wasn't as sharp as before.

"I'm sure sorry, Lonnie. It was a dumb thing I did," Doug said.

"Yes. You could have broken your neck."

"I know. I'm sorry."

"Well, it's over now," Lonnie said.

We didn't talk any more that night. But in the morning when Doug went outside to clean his boots, Lonnie cornered me. "I want to talk to you."

I looked at him and said, "I thought I'd clean my boots, too."

"That can wait, Tricia. I want to know what's the matter with you."

"Nothing," I lied.

"You've been acting strange since yesterday. I saw you coming out of Dunsmuir's den. You talked to him, didn't you?"

"I don't know what you mean," I lied again.

"He told you about Bill Ebbetson, didn't he?"

My stomach tightened. I didn't know if I should try to lie or not. I figured it was no use.

"Sure, he talked to me about it. So what?"

"You tell me, Tricia. We've never gotten along that well. But since yesterday, you've looked at me as if I were a monster."

"No, I don't. But you lied the other night about that painting. You saw that face and you hurt yourself. You lied about all of that."

"You're avoiding my question, Tricia. What did Dunsmuir tell you about Ebbetson?"

"Nothing much. Just that you and he fought."

I headed for the door. I wanted to get out of the cabin. I couldn't stand to be alone with Lonnie for another minute.

He moved in front of the door, blocking my way. "We haven't finished talking. I want to know what Dunsmuir told you."

His voice was low and tense. His eyes clouded over. I was afraid to meet his eyes.

"I told you. He said you had a fight."

"Do you expect me to believe that?"

"You believe anything you want. I'm going outside now." I took another step to the door, but Lonnie refused to move.

"I want to know what he told you."

I looked at him finally. "He told me he knew you when you were a kid. He said you didn't get along with the other kids."

"He told you about Ebbetson and how he died." Lonnie's voice was almost a whisper.

"I'm going outside now."

Lonnie's hand came down and clamped on my wrist. He was short and thin, but he was strong. I'd never imagined he would be so strong.

"Let go of me," I ordered.

"I can tell from your eyes that he told you everything. Now I want you to hear my side of it."

"Well, I don't want to hear it."

"Whether you want to or not, you're going to." With that, Lonnie led me over to a chair and made me sit down.

Beyond the window I saw the snow coming down. Doug was making snowballs and throwing them against the cabin. Every time I heard a thud, I jumped a little.

Lonnie had let go of my arm, but I still felt trapped. I stared down at the rug on the floor, and all the colors ran together.

"Look at me," Lonnie said.

"I don't want to."

He grabbed my chin and forced my face up. "Look at me when I talk to you. You owe me that."

Though I was frightened, I did what he demanded. I saw that he looked angry again.

"I am going to tell you how Bill Ebbetson died."

I stared at those eyes, those tiger eyes. With a shudder, I realized what I'd been suspecting was true. Lonnie's face *was* the face I'd seen in the window. I stared at him, almost hypnotized.

Lonnie's voice was tense when he began. "I'll be honest with you, Tricia, I *was* a disturbed child. Maybe it's because I lost my parents when I was three. Anyway, I was different. I wasn't a healthy, happy kid.

"The people who adopted me took me to all kinds of doctors. Some of them said I was very sick. But none of them really did anything for me."

He paused, struggling with both his pain and anger. Then he continued, "I liked being alone. I hated the other kids. They made fun of me. Can you understand that?"

"Yes," I whispered.

"Well, sometimes I sat for hours watching the birds. Sometimes I painted them, sometimes I just sat and listened. I liked them better than people. At least the birds never made fun of me."

Sweat ran down his face. His entire face shone with it.

"I don't want to hear any more," I protested.

He ignored me. "That day Dunsmuir told you about. I remember it quite clearly, Tricia—how I wish I could forget. I was alone when a bunch of kids snuck up on me. Dunsmuir and Ebbetson and some others.

"I was making bird calls. When they heard me, they started laughing like crazy. How I hated them!

"Then Dunsmuir saw the cardinals. Such beautiful, harmless birds. But not to

Dunsmuir. He shot one of them with his BB gun. I yelled at them all, but they just laughed harder."

Lonnie was breathing hard. The memory twisted his face with pain.

"Then Dunsmuir started to climb a tree to get the cardinals' nest. I pulled him down. He climbed up again and got the nest. I saw it fall. All the baby birds were on the ground, and those damn kids were still laughing.

"That's when I picked up the rock." In spite of herself, Tricia drew in her breath hard. But Lonnie didn't seem to notice.

"I picked it up and went at Dunsmuir. I admit it; *I wanted to hurt him.* For one blinding moment, I felt like bashing his head in.

"Bill Ebbetson saw how mad I was. He tried to pull us apart. But soon we were all fighting—the three of us. We fell and rolled down a hill. Bill hit his head on a rock."

I stared at Lonnie. Was he lying? Or was Mr. Dunsmuir?

"I just stared at Bill. His face looked so

cold and lifeless. Then I saw the blood. I started to scream.

"The next thing I knew, I was in the hospital. They had to strap me down. They said I was crazy."

Lonnie stopped and took a deep breath. "I guess Dunsmuir told you something else."

"He just said the boy was killed."

"I can imagine what he said, Tricia. He said I killed Bill. That's what he told everybody. That was why they kept me in the hospital so long. He lied. The others lied, too. Nobody ever believed what really happened because they all stuck together."

"I'm sorry," I said.

"I suppose you don't believe me either."

"I'm not sure what to believe. I know that you know more about that prowler than you're telling me."

"Maybe. I just don't think you are compassionate enough to handle the truth."

"Compassionate?" I echoed.

"You're a smart girl. You get good grades in school. Don't you know what 'compassionate' means?"

"Yes, of course I do. It means to have pity or sympathy."

Lonnie smiled a strange smile. "Do you have compassion? What if I told you there was a poor, frightened boy out there? Do you think he should be captured?"

"He could be dangerous," I said.

"I thought you'd say that. Maybe your problem isn't compassion, Tricia, but a lack of imagination. You've never been locked up in a terrible place." He stared at me, then looked down at his cupped hands.

"Well, I have," he continued. "It was a hospital. Not a nice children's hospital with cute animals on the wall. It was a terrible place. Always too hot or cold, smelling of every foul odor in the world. No one to really care about us. The people there—if they didn't come in disturbed, the hospital soon did the trick.

"The sad thing was, a lot of us never needed to be hospitalized. We were there basically because we were different. But that terrifies the ordinary people—being different. The ordinary people want to lock away all the different ones."

I began to wonder about Lonnie's plea for compassion. Did he want me to feel sorry for some boy I didn't even know? Or was he asking me to feel sorry for him? Or were they both the same person?

"Don't you think that somebody who is sick should have help?" I asked carefully.

"What kind of help? Being imprisoned in a hospital where the staff is overworked?"

"There must be help somewhere," I said.

"Yes. If people had a little compassion."

Just then the door swung open and Doug stepped inside. "Wow, it's really snowing out there!" he exclaimed.

I looked out the window and saw Doug was right. It was almost a blizzard.

"I bet we get snowed in," Doug said happily.

The thought of that terrified me. I looked at the snow on the ground. It was getting deeper by the minute.

"I've been snowed in here before," Lonnie said. "There's really nothing to worry about. I always keep a lot of canned food on hand. We have plenty of wood, too."

"But doesn't the snowplow come by every day and clear the road?" I asked him.

"No. They don't bother with cabins way out here." He looked at me coldly. "There's still time to drive to the lodge. Would you rather stay there, Tricia?"

Doug stared at us in surprise. "Why would she want to do that, Lonnie?" He looked at me. "You wouldn't, would you?"

"I don't know. It would be more comfortable—"

Doug shook his head. "It'll be fun to be snowed in. We can act like pioneers. Well, you can go to the lodge if you want to, Tricia. I'm staying here with Lonnie."

I desperately wanted to go to the lodge.

But I couldn't leave without Doug. I'd have to persuade him to come along.

I smiled at Doug. "Don't you think you'd have more fun at the lodge? You remember how you loved zipping down those ski slopes—"

"I'm staying here. Let the old blizzard come." Doug laughed.

"I'll drive you to the lodge if you want, Tricia," Lonnie said. "I'm sure your friends, the Dunsmuirs, would be happy to have you there."

I gazed out the window again. In about an hour it would be too late. We would be snowed in. I felt as though some huge trap was slowly sealing shut around me.

I couldn't leave Doug. Quietly I said, "I'll stay."

I looked at my brother. He was smiling happily at the thought of being snowed in. He didn't understand the danger. He didn't understand any of it. In a little while we'd be stuck in the cabin. We didn't even have a phone. It would be just me, Doug—and Lonnie.

8 FROM THE VERY beginning, Doug had liked Lonnie. I'd never understood why. Lonnie was nothing like our dad. Lonnie didn't even understand baseball or football. I remembered the first time he saw us watching a game between the Mets and the Oakland A's.

"Why does that guy keep shaking his head?" Lonnie had asked.

I laughed. "That's the pitcher. He's just signaling the catcher."

Doug and I had tried to explain the rules of the game. But Lonnie really didn't want to learn.

Still, Doug liked him anyway. They had other things in common. For instance, Lonnie helped Doug with his science projects at school. They made a model solar system together.

It pleased Mom to see how well they got along. She was so happy, she never seemed to notice how I felt. I guess she never knew how much I resented Lonnie.

I wondered again if Mom knew about Lonnie's stay in the hospital when he was a boy. Would it have made a difference to her? I thought I knew Mom well, but I wasn't sure how she'd feel about that.

Doug interrupted my train of thoughts. "Wow! Look at that blizzard," he shouted happily. "Hey, Trish, it's piled all over the truck now. I can hardly even see it. It looks like a big white mammoth or something. Hey, Lonnie, come look!"

"I see." Lonnie joined him at the window. He patted Doug on the shoulder.

"You came here a lot before you married Mom, huh, Lonnie?" Doug asked.

"Oh, yes. I loved the solitude."

"What's 'solitude,' Lonnie?"

"Being alone."

"But didn't you get lonely?"

"Sometimes," Lonnie said.

"I would have gotten lonely," Doug said. "Well, you don't have to be lonely anymore, Lonnie. Now you've got us."

Lonnie turned and smiled at Doug. He looked almost handsome.

"Well, I'd better get us ready for the storm," Lonnie said. He quickly fetched more wood in from outside. Then he got out a flashlight and some candles. Doug begged him to light a few. Since he had boxes of the things stored in the cupboard, Lonnie obliged.

The candles made an eerie light in the room. It was worse than the darkness in a way. The wavering flames cast strange shadows on the walls.

Lonnie took out his art supplies. "I think I might paint the storm."

I sat down and watched him. I guess Lonnie was a pretty good artist, but I'd never liked his stuff. I admitted to myself that maybe that was because I didn't like *him*.

"Hey, look," Doug said suddenly. "Something's moving out there."

"Where?" Lonnie asked.

"Maybe it's Tricia's 'friend,' " Doug said.

I looked out the window, too. I couldn't see anything.

"Who would be out on a night like this?" Lonnie asked. He looked nervous, though.

I went to bed at ten. At about eleven, Lonnie got out of his sleeping bag. He got up very slowly. I pretended I was sleeping. He came over to my cot. I could sense him standing over me even though my eyes were closed. Then the floorboards creaked, and I heard him move towards the door.

I dared to open my eyes. I saw Lonnie quietly put on his boots and heavy jacket. Then he moved to the door and opened it. He glanced back once to make sure I was still asleep. Finally he slipped outside.

I heard his boots crunching on the snow. The sound soon faded and then disappeared altogether.

I lay there for a few minutes. Then I got up, too. On tiptoe I crept to the window. The blizzard had stopped. The huge, glowing moon cast an unreal silver light over everything.

Suddenly I heard a sharp cry. It took my breath away for a moment. It must be coyotes yelping at the moon, I hurriedly reassured myself. But I knew the sound was too close for it to be coyotes.

For a minute I couldn't see anything. Then a dark figure suddenly came into view. I dug my fingernails into the palms of my hands.

In the ghostly moonlight, I could see the figure. His eyes gleamed with an eerie, catlike glow. Ice glittered from his dark hair.

"Doug!" I cried. "Doug, come quick!"

"What's the matter?" he answered sleepily.

"Come to the window! Hurry!" I shouted at him. I stared at the figure. Underneath his scanty jacket, I could make out a red and white cotton shirt. It was just the kind of shirt Lonnie wore.

"Doug, hurry!" I screamed. I guess I screamed too loud. The figure jumped, spun around, and ran away.

Doug stumbled to the window. "Where?" he asked.

"You're too late. He's gone."

"Was it that boy?"

"Yeah, he was right out there."

Doug turned toward Lonnie's sleeping bag. "Lonnie! Hey—he's gone."

"I know. He went outside awhile ago, Doug."

Then Doug said something that would have been funny if it weren't so frightening. It was too close to the truth. "Tricia, maybe you just saw Lonnie out there. Could you have seen Lonnie and thought he was that boy?"

"Maybe," I said.

"What's Lonnie doing out there, anyway?"

"I don't know."

Doug stared out the window. "Hey, I see something—it's Lonnie."

"Do you see him now?"

"Yeah. He's over there by the trees. I guess he's looking at the stars."

I doubted that. The sky was still filled with wisps of fast-moving clouds.

"Let's go outside and tell him to come in," Doug said. "It's too cold out there."

"No, Doug, leave him be. Lonnie will

come in when he wants to. If we go out there, he might get mad."

Doug looked at me with surprise. "Why should he get mad?"

"Because. Come on, go back to bed."

"Tricia, you're really acting strange. What's the matter with you?" Doug asked angrily. He was always angry when awakened out of a deep sleep. "You know what I think? I think you're just mad because Lonnie married Mom. You sure are nasty to Lonnie sometimes."

"Don't be silly," I said, but I hoped Doug couldn't see the confusion on my face.

I turned to the window and looked out again. I couldn't see Lonnie anymore. I wondered if Doug had seen him at all. Maybe he saw the boy from the back and just thought it was Lonnie.

Reluctantly, I asked him, "Doug, are you sure you saw Lonnie?"

"Sure I am."

"Did you actually see his *face*?"

"I know Lonnie even when I don't see his face," Doug said. He went to the stove. "I'm going to make some tea.

Lonnie will want some when he comes in."

I stared out into the darkness and wondered. Would Lonnie be the same person when he came back to the cabin? Or would he be someone we barely recognized, someone terrible?

I walked over to Doug in the kitchen. "Doug, I want to go out and talk to Lonnie."

"I'll come, too," he volunteered.

"No. I want to talk to him alone."

"Oh," he sounded puzzled. "Sure, okay."

I had to find out what happened. Lonnie would never tell the truth with Doug standing there. I buttoned my jacket and went outside.

"You looking for something?" Lonnie's voice came from back in the trees.

"For you," I said.

He came into the clearing. "You shouldn't be out here."

"Then what are you doing out here?" I quickly shot back.

Lonnie didn't answer me. He simply stared off in the distance for a moment.

Then he sighed and walked back to the cabin. I followed him inside.

"Hey, Lonnie," Doug cheerfully greeted him. "I made some tea for you. Did Trish tell you that she saw that kid again?"

Lonnie merely grunted. But he thanked Doug for the tea and settled at the table to sip it. With a sleepy good night, Doug went back to bed.

I sat at the table with Lonnie. After a few minutes had passed and we could hear Doug's steady breathing, Lonnie quietly spoke.

"So you saw something tonight?"

"Yes. The same thing I saw before."

Lonnie stared down into his mug of tea. Then he looked up, directly into my eyes. "His name is Michael."

"*What?*" I nearly shouted in astonishment.

"Shhh. You'll wake Doug. The boy—his name is Michael."

"Who is he? Where's he from?"

"He's a runaway from a private hospital for disturbed children. Right now, he's living in a cave. I've seen him several times. Every time we meet, he's friendlier. He told me his name is Michael."

I stared at Lonnie. Why was he telling me all this now? Did he know I suspected that he and the boy were the same person? Was he trying to divert my suspicion with this lie? Or did Michael really exist?

"How long ago did he escape?" I asked Lonnie. I had to pretend I believed him. Part of me did anyway.

"A year ago. He says he lives on berries, fish, small things he steals from empty cabins. Tricia, he's frightened. He's just a sick, frightened boy."

"Why didn't you tell me this right away?"

"Because I didn't think you were compassionate enough. You'd think he should be captured and taken away," Lonnie said.

"So you feel it's better that he's out here living like a wild animal?" I asked.

Lonnie's eyes flared with anger. "Better than screaming at white walls? Better than being put in a straitjacket? Yes, I do think so!"

He stood up and paced a little. Then he took a deep breath and sat down at the table again. When he spoke, he seemed calmer.

"I don't want him to live out here forever either, Tricia. I know a couple in California who help kids like Michael. If I could get Michael to trust me, I could take him there. He would have a chance with them." His voice was soft and pleading as though he were arguing a case before me.

"I just don't want him trapped like a wild animal. That's why I don't want anybody to know about him."

"I see," I said.

Lonnie sat back and watched me. "I suppose you want to report Michael, now that you know," he said.

"I won't if you don't want me to," I said.

"He's not dangerous, Tricia. In fact, he's really gentle."

I looked at Lonnie. "You were gentle, too, weren't you?"

A strange look came into his eyes. "Why did you say that?"

"I don't know. It just occurred to me, that's all."

He looked suspicious. "What are you *really* thinking, Tricia?"

"Nothing. In fact, I'm too tired to think. I'm going to bed." With that I got up and went over to my cot. Lonnie soon sought out his own sleeping bag.

Strange to say after such a wild night, I slept very well.

The next morning I was up pretty early. I hurried outside to see if there were any footprints still left in the snow. If I found another set of prints besides my own and Lonnie's, that would prove somebody else had been in the clearing last night. But the wind had wiped out all signs of tracks.

As I turned to go back into the cabin, I heard an engine. It was Ben, skimming over the drifts in a snowmobile.

As he drew closer, he shouted, "I was worried about you last night."

"We're okay." I gave him a big smile to prove it.

Ben pulled up and killed the motor.

"The weatherman says another storm is coming. Maybe you really should come to the lodge with me." His eyes were hopeful.

Ben's offer was tempting. I wanted to tell him about Michael and my doubts about Lonnie. Yet what Lonnie had told me was private. So I just smiled at Ben and shook my head.

"Tricia, Dad and I were talking last night. We really think—"

I cut him off. "We're fine, Ben. Don't worry."

He got off the snowmobile and came across the snow to where I stood. He reached out and took my hand. "Tricia, please. I *care* about you."

It felt good being close to Ben. I loved his dark, laughing eyes and friendly grin. He was such a wonderful, ordinary person. No secrets, no dark corners. I think that if Mom had married a man like Ben, I wouldn't have minded so much.

Maybe what Lonnie had said was true after all. I couldn't accept people who were *different*.

"I'm glad you care, Ben. And I care

about you, too," I said.

Doug came outside then. Ben offered him a ride on the snowmobile, and Doug quickly darted back into the cabin to get permission. When Lonnie said he could go, Doug came running out. The snowmobile went roaring away over the snow.

I went back inside the cabin. Lonnie looked at me with suspicion. But I was getting used to that. Now he never looked at me any other way.

"Did you tell Ben about Michael?" he softly demanded.

"No," I took off my coat. "I said I wouldn't, didn't I?"

"But I don't trust you."

"Well, that makes us even. I don't trust you either," I said.

"Have you ever trusted me?" Lonnie asked.

I hesitated. "I guess not."

"You wish I'd never married your mother, don't you? That I was completely out of your life."

Lonnie looked hurt, but I was tired of his excuses and self-pity. He'd hurt me plenty, too. Did he ever think of that?

"That's right," I said. I didn't even try to hide my bitterness.

Our eyes met for a moment. Lonnie finally realized what I'd known from the start. We were enemies.

9 I FELT DEEPLY grateful when the sound of Ben's returning snowmobile interrupted us. Soon Doug and Ben came charging into the house, shaking the snow from their boots.

"Man, that was fun!" Doug shouted.

Lonnie managed a smile. "Want some breakfast, Ben? We have enough to go around."

"I was thinking maybe Tricia might come back to the lodge with me," Ben said.

"Up to her," Lonnie said.

"No, Ben, I don't think so," I replied.

"Well, then, want to change your mind and stay for breakfast?" Lonnie asked again.

"Thanks, I will," Ben said.

Lonnie soon had some rolls and ham slices served up for everybody. Ben and Doug dug in eagerly, but I only picked at my food. I was too upset to enjoy it.

"Another big storm coming," Ben said

between bites. "Why don't you all come to the lodge?"

"We'll be fine here," Lonnie said.

"Sure," Doug agreed.

Ben asked cautiously, "Seen anything more of your prowler?"

"No," I said.

"I've got to admit, I'd be a little worried if I were stuck up here. It's just so isolated—could be dangerous," Ben warned.

"I've never had any trouble here, and I don't expect to now," Lonnie said firmly.

"But, Mr. Boone, what if a prowler should break in?" Ben looked right at Lonnie.

"Are you afraid of prowlers, Ben?" Lonnie asked. "I thought you and your dad were so brave."

Ben put down his fork and leaned back. But he didn't say anything. I could see he was holding his temper for my sake.

When he finally spoke, he changed the subject entirely. "Dad asked me to pick up the skis he loaned Doug."

"Good luck finding them," Lonnie said.

"They're under twenty feet of snow by now."

"I'm really sorry, Ben," Doug said. "See, we had an accident—"

"No need to lie," Lonnie cut in. "I left them out there on purpose. You tell your father that's what he can expect when he doesn't mind his own business."

Ben stared in shock at Lonnie. At last he got up and said, "Thanks for the breakfast. I think I'll go look for those skis now. Maybe Tricia can show me where they are."

"No," Lonnie said. "It's a good distance from here. I don't want her walking that far if another storm is coming on.

Ben looked very angry, but he still didn't lash back at Lonnie. "Well, would you mind if Tricia and I just stepped outside for a minute?"

"No, go ahead," Lonnie said.

I silently followed Ben out of the cabin. We walked a short distance and then stopped near a lovely snow-covered pine.

"I'm really worried, Tricia," Ben said. "Lonnie has been acting awfully strange."

"He's just upset, that's all," I said.

"Look, Tricia, he once *killed* a boy when he was upset."

I shook my head. "He told me a different story."

"I'm not surprised," Ben replied.

"He said Bill Ebbetson's death was an accident."

"Did you think he would tell you the truth, Tricia?"

The image of Lonnie's eyes as he told the story suddenly came to my mind. "Ben, how do you know the truth? It happened before we were born. A bunch of kids were fighting. Who knows who lied?"

Ben looked unhappy. "Tricia, I know my dad. He always tells the truth. And I know that your stepfather was hospitalized. I can't help but worry about you and Doug being here alone with him."

"I appreciate how you feel, Ben. But I can't go with you. It would be like declaring war on Lonnie. Then Mom would have to choose between me and him. It would break her heart!"

Ben reached out and pulled me into his

arms. The comfort of his hug made me realize how lonely and weary I was.

"Oh, Ben—I do want to go with you—"

"Then come."

"I can't," I said, pulling away from him. I turned quickly and ran back to the cabin.

The rest of the morning at the cabin, we were all pretty quiet. I read and wrote letters to friends. Lonnie got out his painting gear and gave Doug lessons.

In the afternoon, Doug began to feel housebound. The storm still hadn't rolled in, so Lonnie went outside with Doug and built a snowman. I sat on a log and watched as they tied a red scarf around the snowman's neck. Then Lonnie created a peaked witch's hat from aluminum foil. Finally they made big shiny eyes out of aluminum pie plates and a nose from a carrot.

All the time they were working, they laughed and tossed snow at each other. They were just like two kids.

"Isn't it a great snowman?" Doug shouted.

"Sure," I said.

Later on, when I was alone with Doug, he asked, "What's the matter with you? You used to be a lot of fun. Now you never laugh or smile."

"You wouldn't understand," I said. It was a dumb thing to say. I always hated it when people said that to me.

"Oh, I understand," Doug said. "You just hate Lonnie, that's all. You're jealous of him. You never wanted him to marry Mom. You were the big shot in our house after Dad died. Then Lonnie came, and now you're not the big shot anymore."

"Doug, that's not true," I said. But to myself, I was forced to admit that there might be some truth in what he said. Maybe a lot of truth.

"Lonnie tries so hard to be nice. He's a great guy. Why can't you be nice to him?"

"Oh, Doug—"

"I bet you made up that whole prowler story just to force us to go home. You wanted to spoil this trip."

"Doug, Lonnie saw the boy, too. He did!" It was out before I knew what I was saying. I'd promised Lonnie to keep quiet about the boy. Now here I was blurting out the news at the first opportunity.

"He did? I don't believe you. I'm going to ask him," Doug said.

"No, don't! Please, Doug, I promised not to tell anybody!"

But Doug was already running into the cabin. "Hey, Lonnie, Tricia says you saw the boy, too. Did you?"

Lonnie looked at me. Then he calmly put down his paint brushes and walked over to Doug. "Yes. But, Doug, you must promise not to say anything to anybody if I tell you about him. It'll be our secret, okay?"

Doug's eyes grew big. "Sure, Lonnie!"

We all moved over to the fireplace and sat down. Lonnie began his explanation in a quiet voice. "The prowler your sister saw was a teenage boy named Michael. He ran away from a hospital because he felt frightened—and lonely and confused. Right now, he's living off the land—and stealing from cabins. I'm trying to help him—to be his friend."

Doug looked serious. "Yeah?"

"If others found out about Michael, he might be in danger. They might try to hunt him down and capture him. You can imagine how that would terrify him. He might even be injured. You understand, don't you, Doug?"

"Sure, Lonnie. So what does he *really* look like?"

"Like a frightened kid, I suppose. But he's not like you, Doug. He was born with certain problems. That's why people have abused him sometimes. Not everyone has the compassion to deal with a troubled boy like Michael." Lonnie glanced at me.

"I bet I could make friends with him," Doug said.

Lonnie smiled. "I bet you could, too, Doug."

"Maybe you could let me meet him?"

"Maybe. But listen, Doug—not right away. In fact, if you should see him, don't go near him. I accidentally startled him one night, and he scratched my arm. He didn't mean to. He's just very frightened. So you mustn't tell anybody about Michael. Okay?"

"I swear I won't, Lonnie," Doug said.

Doug believed the whole story. He loved and respected Lonnie so much that he always believed him. Sometimes it seemed to me that Lonnie was more of a father to Doug than Dad had been. Dad was always away flying planes. Lonnie, on the other hand, acted as a companion and teacher. I suddenly envied Doug.

Doug and I took a walk before supper. As we trudged through the snow, he said to me, "Isn't it great the way Lonnie is trying to help that poor kid? Most people wouldn't care about somebody like Michael."

I didn't say anything.

"Tricia, how come you don't like him?" Doug asked me. I stared into his soft brown eyes. Doug seemed very old, for twelve. The little boy face was going away, and he was starting to look like Dad. In a way, I was sorry to see that change.

"I don't know, Doug. I just can't trust him."

Doug walked away without saying anything.

I stared up at the sky. All the blue was gone. Thick, smoky clouds were racing overhead, choking off the light.

The last rays of the sun fell on the snowman. I stared at it. It had looked funny before; now it seemed evil. The pie plate eyes appeared to glow angrily. The mouth curved in a sneer.

I shrugged off the silly thought. I only wished I could shake off the feeling that something evil was closing in around me.

10

AFTER SUPPER, WE lit candles again. The warmth and soft light of the cabin might have given me a cozy feeling in a different situation. But now, as I listened to the gusting wind and snow outside, I felt trapped.

I sat by the window thinking about Doug's question. Just why didn't I like Lonnie?

I ran off all the reasons in my mind. It was like making a grocery list. He was too short. He had a funny voice. He laughed too much. He sang off-key. He painted weird pictures. He hated sports—he didn't even know what a free throw was.

Finally I had to admit to myself that none of those reasons mattered. What really mattered was that Lonnie had married Mom. I wasn't the most important person in her life anymore.

Doug had been right all along. I was jealous of Lonnie.

But now it was more than that. I was honestly afraid of him, too.

I cautiously glanced over at Lonnie. He was listening to classical music on his MP3 player. His eyes were closed, and he seemed lost in the music.

I turned in early that night and slept pretty well. The blizzard stopped sometime before morning. When I woke, everything was very still.

I hadn't heard Lonnie go out during the night. But I spotted his wet boots by the door, so I figured he must have gone out.

Just after I finished dressing, Ben came by in his snowmobile. I went outside to talk to him.

"You okay, Tricia?" he asked.

"Sure. You look upset. What's wrong?"

"Another family—the Harrisons— saw your prowler last night. In fact, the prowler broke their window. They were nearly frightened to death," Ben said.

Lonnie and Doug had followed me outside and overheard Ben's news.

"What happened exactly?" Lonnie asked.

"The kid broke a window and got into the Harrisons' bedroom," Ben said coldly. "Tried to kill them."

"You don't know that," Lonnie said. He seemed very nervous. "Whoever it was, why he was probably just trying to steal some food."

"You seem very interested in this prowler, Mr. Boone," Ben's voice was hard. "Do you know something we don't know?"

Lonnie hesitated for a moment. Then he admitted, "I've seen him. He's just a frightened runaway boy."

Ben laughed sharply. "The Harrisons said he looked pretty savage to them. They said he had fiery eyes and darted around like an animal. I think we've got a madman on the loose, Mr. Boone—a madman who could end up killing somebody."

"They were probably just upset. That boy isn't a madman, and he's not going to kill anybody. Give me a few days. I'll find him," Lonnie said.

"No way," Ben snapped. "It's too late for that. Dad and I and some other people at the lodge are getting a search party together right now. We're going to get that madman before he kills someone."

"For heaven's sake, Ben, he's scared out of his mind!" Lonnie shouted. "You could hurt him tracking him down like this!"

"That depends on him," Ben said sharply. He went back to his snowmobile. He seemed excited.

I suddenly recalled a picture I'd seen of a soldier preparing for battle. There was the same gleam in the soldier's eyes and Ben's. That look seemed both frightening and awful. Yet there was something exciting about it, too.

Then I remembered what Lonnie had said. He'd warned me about people like the Dunsmuirs—*violent people who let their emotions get the better of them.*

When Ben was gone, Doug turned to Lonnie. "What are you going to do?"

"I'm going with them. Maybe I can stop them from hurting Michael," Lonnie said determinedly.

"Do you think they'll find him?" Doug asked.

"I don't know."

Lonnie went inside the house to get his heavy jacket. I followed him. Before he took off, I had to ask him the question that had been haunting me for so long.

"Lonnie, is there really a Michael?" I asked.

He stopped and whirled towards me. "What?"

"Is there really a Michael?"

"Of course there is. Who do you think you saw?"

I was trembling, but I had to say it. "Maybe I saw you."

I'm not sure how to describe Lonnie's reaction. He might have been amazed or angry. He stared at me for a moment, his mouth open and his eyes wide.

Then he put on his jacket and went to the door. He looked at me once before he went out. But he didn't say a word.

As he closed the door, the feeling rushed over me that something terrible was about to happen. It seemed to me that if they shot the boy, Lonnie would die.

I broke into a run and tore out of the

house after Lonnie. I caught up to him and shouted, "I'm coming with you."

He looked at me in surprise. Before he could say a word, Doug chimed in, "Me, too."

Lonnie started to protest. Then he looked from my face to Doug's. With a shrug, he gave in.

We helped Lonnie put chains on the truck and then drove to the lodge. The truck had four-wheel drive, so we made it through the deep snow.

By the time we reached the lodge, the search party was ready to take off. I saw Sheriff Somers there, along with Mr. Dunsmuir. Altogether there were about a dozen people.

Lonnie got out of the truck and slowly walked towards the group. He stopped in front of the sheriff. "Is the hunting party all ready?" he asked in a bitter voice.

"Come on, Lonnie," Sheriff Somers objected. "That madman has to be caught. You know it as well as I do."

"He's only a frightened runaway kid," Lonnie said.

Just then I noticed Ben at the back of the crowd. I caught his eye and he came over.

"Ben, please, no shooting," I begged him.

"You know I wouldn't do anything like that unless I had to. You trust me, don't you?" He took my hand.

"Yes, I trust you, Ben," I said. But all I could see was the rifle he carried.

The search party took off, with Lonnie along. Though Doug and I wanted to go with them, Lonnie refused. So we sat in the lodge, worrying. I prayed that there would be no shooting.

They returned in the late afternoon, cold and angry. They hadn't found Michael. Lonnie was the only one who seemed happy.

Mr. Dunsmuir spoke to me privately. "Your stepfather seems to know a lot about this madman—a lot that he's not saying. He kept getting in our way out there."

"He made everybody mad," Ben added. "He wanted to know if the safety was set on each rifle. Then he kept wanting to stop and rest. It was pretty clear to everybody that he was trying to stop us from finding the prowler."

The sheriff approached then and spoke to the Dunsmuirs. They agreed to try again the next day. With that, the searchers separated.

Lonnie drove us back to the cabin. He was in high spirits. "They couldn't find anything," he said with a chuckle.

"I'm glad they didn't find Michael," Doug said.

"So am I." Lonnie smiled. "You should have been there, Doug. They were plowing through snowdrifts, stumbling around. The way they handle guns, I was afraid we'd all get shot."

I think we all felt relieved that night when we returned to the cabin. But we were fools to forget how fearful the Dunsmuirs and many of the other residents were.

That night Mr. Dunsmuir and Ben and two other men started searching again. They didn't tell anybody—not even the sheriff. I think they felt sure they could find the prowler on their own.

The night was clear and cold. It was so cold, the air seemed to crackle. We were all sitting in the cabin. Lonnie was painting.

Suddenly he stood up and moved to the door. "I heard something."

"What?" Doug and I both asked.

"Listen!"

We sat very still and strained our ears. Then we all heard it. There were some people outside, tramping through the snow. Suddenly a dog yelped. We probably all realized the same thing at once: the searchers were out again, this time with bloodhounds.

Lonnie's face twisted with pain. Then he cried, "Those fools!" He struggled into his jacket with desperate energy.

"Lonnie, let me come with you," Doug pleaded.

"No!" He threw on his boots and rushed out the door. I watched him race across the blue-white snow.

For a moment I stood there thinking.

What if he and the boy were the same person? The dogs would run him down. The men might even shoot him!

I hurriedly put on my jacket and boots. "Doug, please stay here," I said.

But Doug was dressing, too. He couldn't stay in the cabin. He couldn't any more than I could.

We rushed to the milky clearing and both saw it at the same time. The dogs, still on their leashes, were going crazy. They had the scent of the boy. The men with guns were moving quickly, a wild excitement in their faces.

Then I saw the boy. He was crouching in the clearing, his back to a tree. His eyes were huge and terrified.

I grabbed Doug's arm. "There he is!"

A look of pure agony passed over Doug's face. "Tricia—oh, Tricia."

I could make out what the boy was saying then. "Mich-ael, Mich-ael—" He was sobbing out the word. "Mich-ael."

The dogs were almost uncontrollable now. They leapt in the air and barked savagely.

"He's mad!" Mr. Dunsmuir shouted.

I looked desperately around for Lonnie, but I didn't see him anywhere. "Oh, no, no," I whispered. I couldn't stop the tears from running down my face.

The men with the guns were closing in. "Oh, my God," I cried. I saw their faces as Lonnie had seen them, full of violence and eager for the kill. They seemed on fire with something as old and awful as hate and war.

"Don't hurt him!" I shouted.

Then I met Ben's eyes. For a moment we looked at each other.

"He's a madman," someone shouted.

"No! Please!" I begged.

The boy suddenly picked up a branch of wood and hurled it. I think he lunged at the men, but I can't be sure.

I saw a gun raised: Mr. Dunsmuir's gun. Knowing I'd be too late, I still dashed forward. But then someone reached for the barrel and shoved the gun upward.

The gun went off. I stared in horror as the boy cried out and staggered. He held his arm where a red spot grew.

Then Lonnie was there. He stood between the hunters and the boy. It was like a double-exposed film. Lonnie's image and the boy's seemed to blend together. As the boy fell, Lonnie fell.

"Lonnie!" I screamed, running to him.

With a rush of relief, I saw Lonnie hadn't been shot after all. He was just kneeling by the boy.

I stared at the two of them. The *two* of them. For the first time I was really sure there was a Michael.

Lonnie gently lifted Michael and held him in his arms. Ben put down his rifle and came over.

"You'll be okay, Michael," Lonnie said softly. He looked at Ben. "The shot just grazed him. You saved him, Ben."

I realized then that it had been Ben who'd pushed the gun out of the way. I was so glad he'd tried to stop his father from shooting.

Tears were running down Lonnie's face, but I didn't think it was weak of him. It was funny, but I realized that Lonnie had taught me something very important. He'd shown me that being a man wasn't about being tall, or fearless, or athletic. No, being a good man—or woman—meant you had compassion and the courage to stand up for what you believed in. And those were qualities I should respect and even try to imitate.

I watched as the other men moved in and clumsily tried to bundle up Michael. A sense of shame seemed to have overcome them all. They were now quiet—even gentle.

As they bound Michael's arm, I stared at my ghost boy. He seemed so ordinary lying there, just like any other fifteen-year-old kid. He didn't look like a monster at all.

A longing to help him rushed over me. I knew that if we all worked together, we might be able to ease some of the horror of his life.

That's what Lonnie had been trying to do all along. I looked at my stepfather as he stood up and directed the men to carry Michael into our cabin. When he moved to follow them, I stepped forward.

"Lonnie," I called. He stopped and we stared at each other.

"Please forgive me," I begged.

I guess I wanted to be forgiven for all the mean things I'd said to him. I wanted to apologize for all the times I'd resented him and hadn't believed him. I knew now he'd told the truth about everything— even Bill Ebbetson.

Lonnie moved closer and opened his arms. There was room for me in his arms. There always had been.